The HUNGRY GOAT

Alan Mills Illustrated by **Abner Graboff**

There was a man,
Now please take note,
There was a man
Who had a goat.
He loved that goat,
Indeed he did!
He loved that goat
Just like a kid!

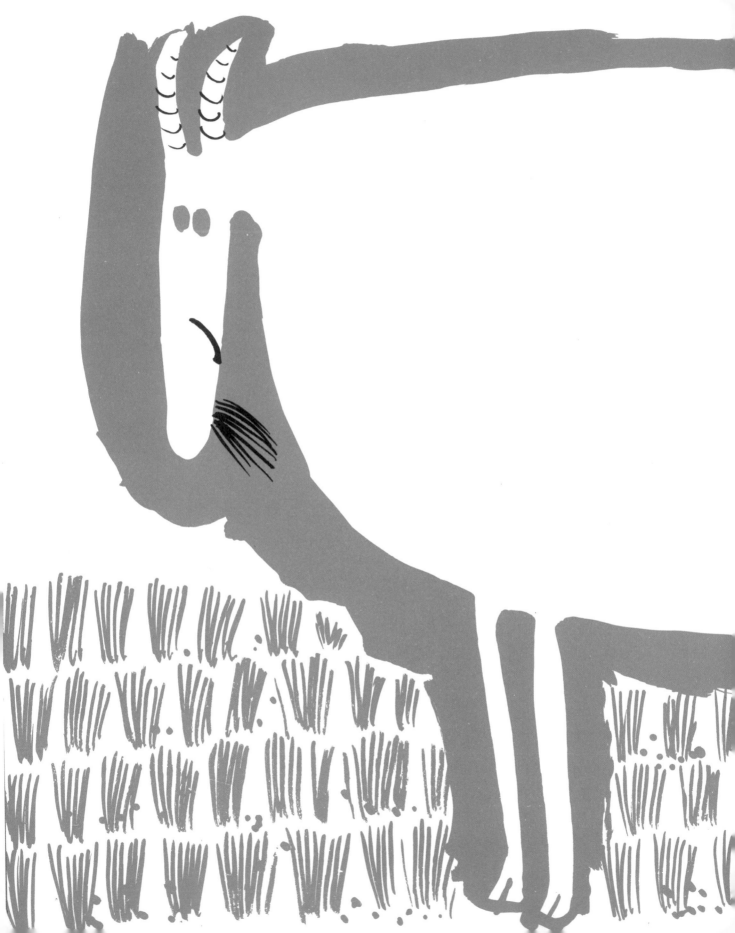

That goat was born,
So I've heard said,
With two small horns
Upon his head.
He had a beard
Upon his chin,
And the whitest coat
You've ever seen.

When he was young
He was so small,
You'd hardly think
He ate at all.
But he ate so much,
It was a fright!
No one could touch
His appetite!

All day he chewed
And chewed and chewed,
For all he saw
He thought was food.

He nibbled grass,

And leaves and twigs,

And even stole
The swill from pigs!

He swallowed flies,
And bugs and bees,

And chewed the bark
Of many trees,

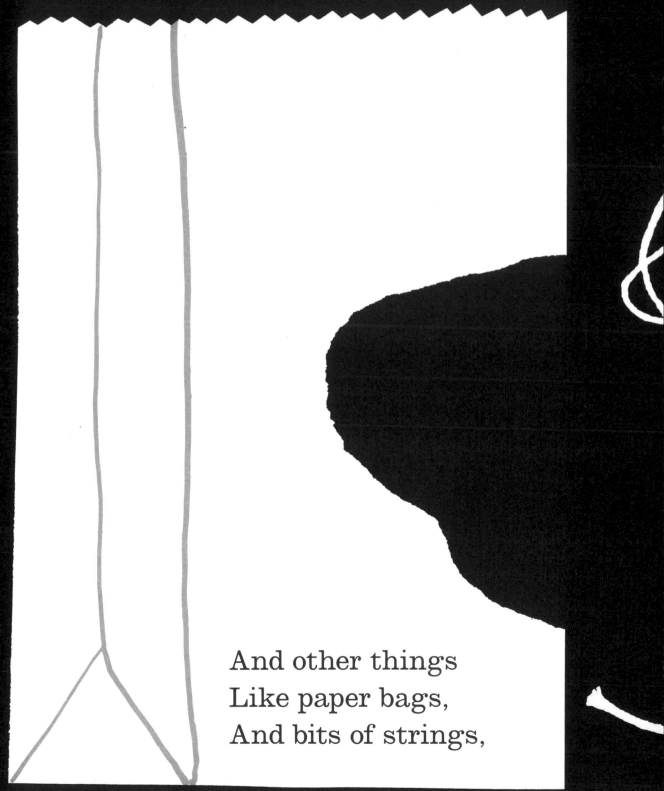

And other things
Like paper bags,
And bits of strings,

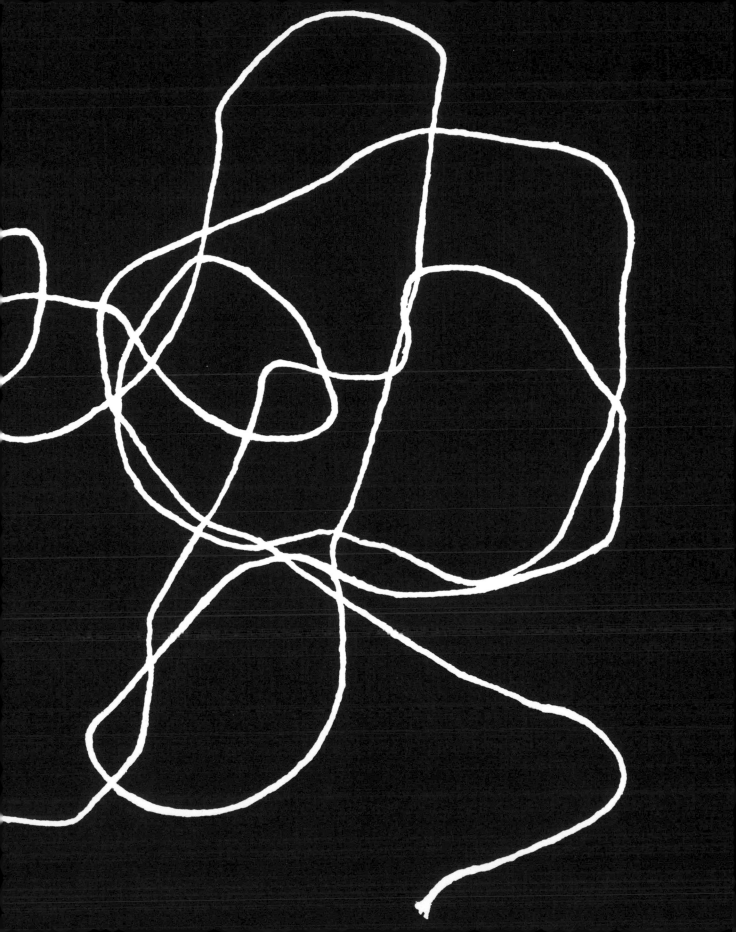

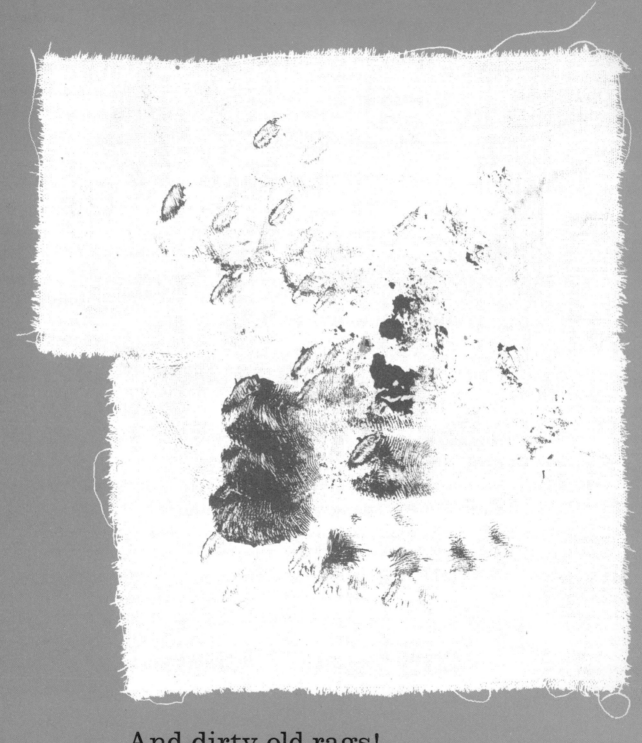

And dirty old rags!

And chicken feathers,

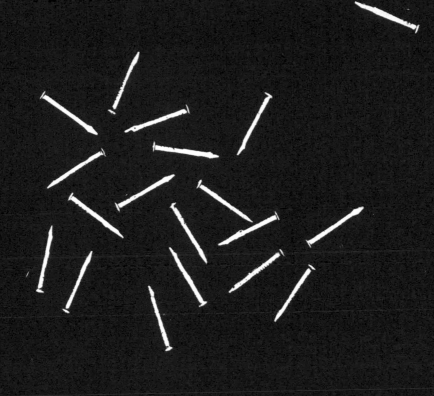

And flour sacks,

And old shoe leather,
Complete with tacks!

And rubber tires
From used-up cars,

And broken glass
From bottles and jars!

Though you may think
That I'm a liar,
I swear he loved
To eat barbed wire!

And rusty nails,

And old tin cans,

And pots and pails,
And frying pans!

Now that there goat,
He grew and grew,
Until he reached
Just five-feet two!
But still he grew
And grew some more,
Until he got
To six-feet four!

His master rode
Him everywhere,
To rodeos
And county fairs.
He always won
The biggest prize,
For there was none
To match his size.

His master was
So proud of him;
He was so proud,
It was a sin!
Then trouble came
And he got mad,
And what he did
Was very sad!

That hungry goat,
One morning fine,
Ate three red shirts
From off the line!
His master grabbed
Him by the back,
And tied him to
A railroad track!

Now when the train
Came into sight,
That goat became
Pale-green with fright!
He heaved a sigh,
As if in pain;
Coughed up those shirts
And flagged the train!

Now when the train
Came to a stop,
The engineer
Called for a cop!
They took that goat
To the county jail,
And there they held
Him without bail!

While waiting there
To hear his fine,
That hungry goat
Began to pine.
For all he got
To eat each day
Was a bit of straw
Or dried-up hay.

His hunger grew
Till, with a moan,
He began to chew
That wall of stone!
He chewed and chewed
Clean through the wall,
And thus escaped
And fooled them all!

The goat, he ran
Without a stop,
Until he came
To a bak'ry shop;
And there he saw
Before his eyes
A pile of dough
Set out to rise.

Now of that dough
He had a feast.
How could he know
'Twas full of yeast?

And when the dough
Began to rise,
That goat blew up
To twice his size!

He looked just like
A big balloon,
As he floated off,
Bound for the moon!

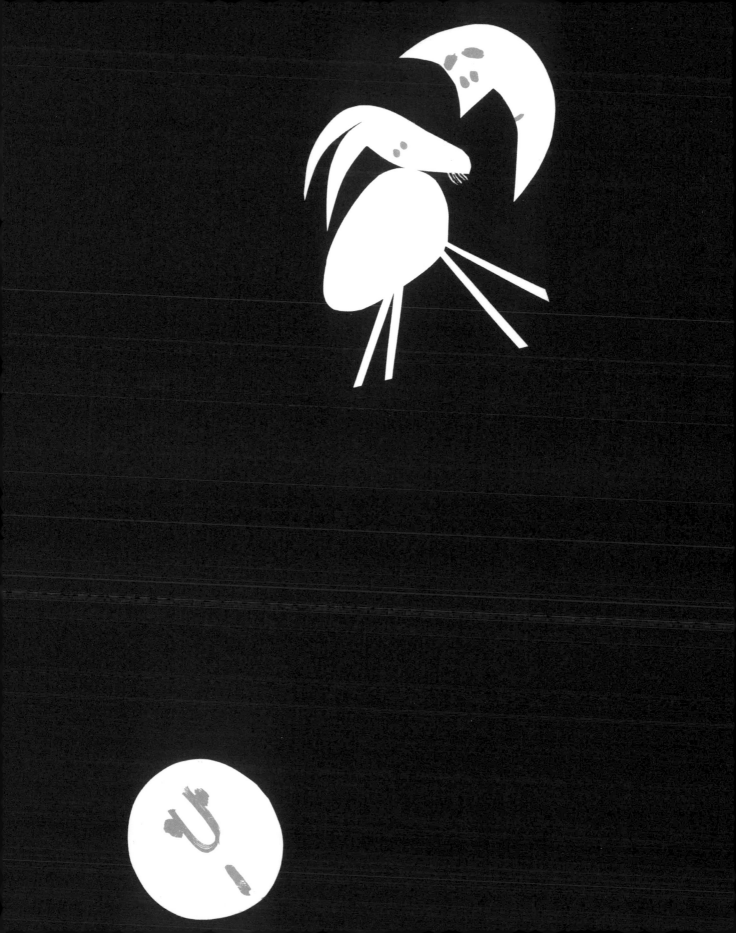

Now of this tale,
This is the end,
For no one saw
That goat again!

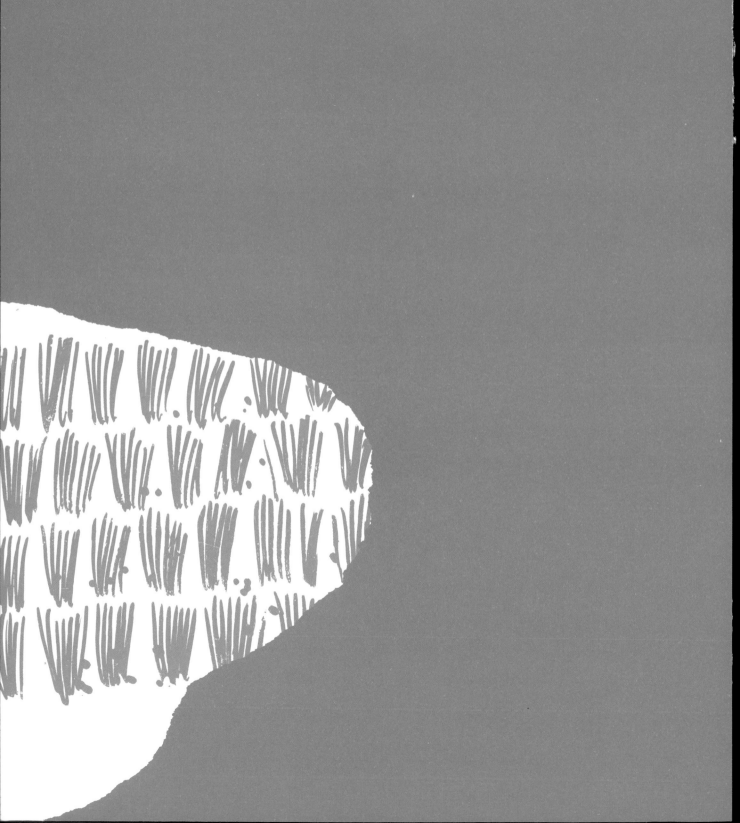